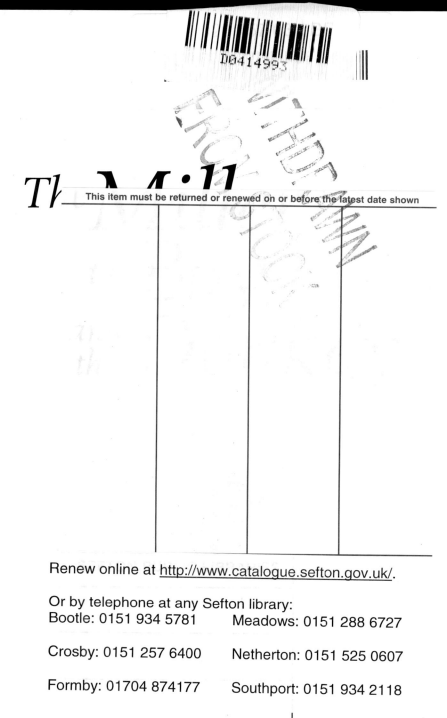

Th **M· 11**

This item must be returned or renewed on or before the latest date shown

Renew online at http://www.catalogue.sefton.gov.uk/.

Or by telephone at any Sefton library:

Bootle: 0151 934 5781   Meadows: 0151 288 6727

Crosby: 0151 257 6400   Netherton: 0151 525 0607

Formby: 01704 874177   Southport: 0151 934 2118

A fine will be charged on any overdue item plus the cost of reminders sent

For all children, young and old.

OXFORD
UNIVERSITY PRESS

Great Clarendon Street, Oxford OX2 6DP

Oxford University Press is a department of the University of Oxford.
It furthers the University's objective of excellence in research, scholarship,
and education by publishing worldwide in

Oxford   New York

Auckland   Cape Town   Dar es Salaam   Hong Kong   Karachi
Kuala Lumpur   Madrid   Melbourne   Mexico City   Nairobi
New Delhi   Shanghai   Taipei   Toronto

With offices in
Argentina   Austria   Brazil   Chile   Czech Republic   France   Greece
Guatemala   Hungary   Italy   Japan   Poland   Portugal   Singapore
South Korea   Switzerland   Thailand   Turkey   Ukraine   Vietnam

Oxford is a registered trade mark of Oxford University Press
in the UK and in certain other countries

First published 1969
First published in paperback 1983
Reissued in paperback 1999
This new edition first published in paperback 2008

British Library Cataloguing in Publication Data
Data available

ISBN: 978-0-19-272091-7 (paperback)

1 3 5 7 9 10 8 6 4 2

Printed in China

Brian Wildsmith

The Miller, the Boy, and the Donkey

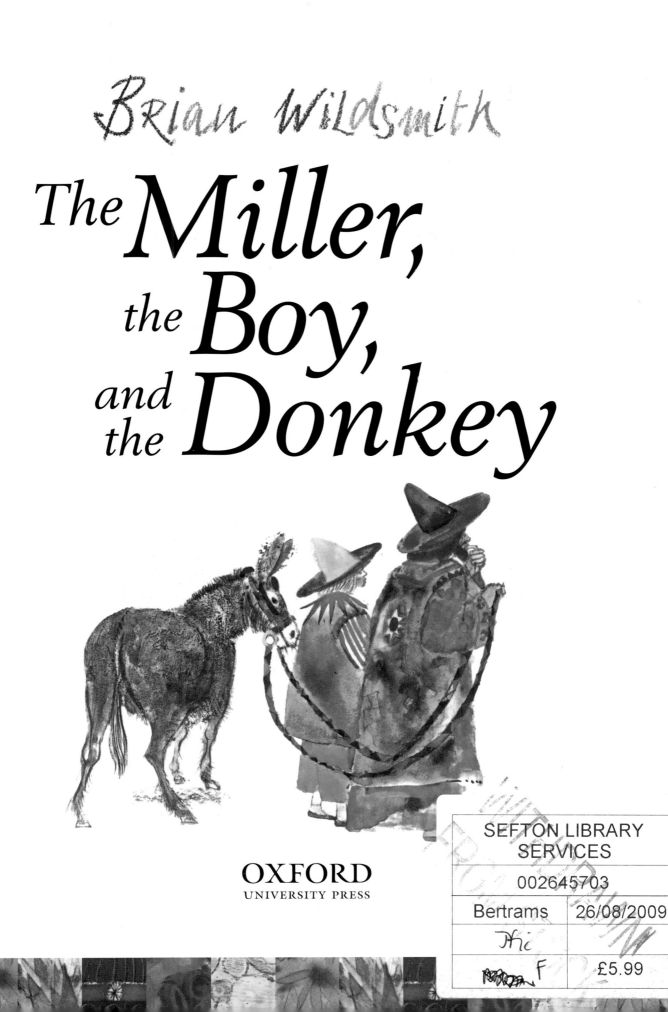

OXFORD

UNIVERSITY PRESS

One fine morning the miller decided to take his donkey to market and sell him.

So he and his boy
went into the field
to catch him.

They took with them some carrots which the donkey loved to eat. *Sure enough* when he saw the carrots the donkey came trotting towards them.

When he had eaten the carrots they took him to the
mill and brushed his coat and polished his hooves and
combed his mane. He looked so *smart* and *clean*
the miller decided to *carry* him to market to save
him from dirtying his feet on the way.

They had not gone very far before they met
a farmer.

He burst out laughing when he saw them. *'How silly you are,'* he cried. 'Fancy carrying a donkey! Why he should be carrying you, not you carrying him.'

The miller did not like to be laughed at,

so he made the donkey start walking.

Then the boy began to feel tired and the miller
lifted him on to the donkey's back.

A little further on they met three merchants who were angry when they saw the boy riding while the miller walked.

'*Why you lazy lad,*' they said. 'Get down
from the donkey and let the old man ride.'

The miller made the boy get down and he himself

climbed on to the donkey's back. But it was very hot
and the boy soon became tired again.

After a while they met three girls. '*Shame on you master,*' they called out. 'How can you ride at ease while your poor boy limps so wearily behind?'

So the miller told the boy to climb up behind him and they both rode on the donkey.

Before long they saw a priest standing outside his church. He rebuked the miller sternly. 'It is cruel for both of you to ride on the back of this little animal. *Have you no pity* for such a faithful beast?'

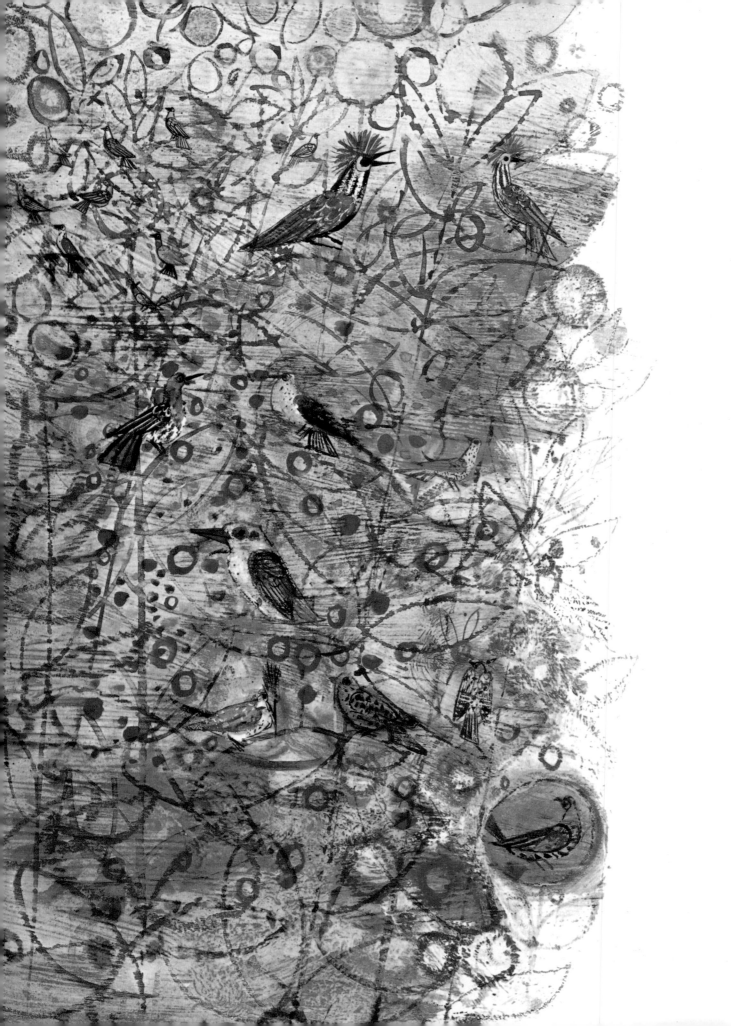

With a sigh the miller climbed down and lifted the boy off the donkey. Wearily they plodded along in the hot sun with the donkey trotting gaily beside them.

At last they came to the market-place. All the people were amused to see the miller and his boy trudging along in the heat of the sun, when they might have ridden on their donkey. *'The miller is crazy,'* they said.

The miller sold his donkey quite quickly to a kind farmer. But his head ached from thinking about his **difficult journey** and all the different kinds of advice he had received.

'From now on,' he confided to his boy, 'I shall make up *my own mind* and stick to it.'

The boy thought this would be an excellent idea. He nodded his head, and yawned, and they went in search of their dinner.